Dear Abel,

Never give up on a dream
And always reach for the
stars.

God Bless,
Peace & Love
Mario

Children of Flight
PEDRO PAN

Maria Armengol Acierno

SILVER MOON PRESS

CHILDREN OF FLIGHT PEDRO PAN
Maria Armengol Acierno

First Silver Moon Press Edition 1994

The publisher would like to thank Professor Robert M. Levine
of the University of Miami for his help in preparing
the Historical Postscript.

For information contact
Silver Moon Press,
126 Fifth Avenue
Suite 803
New York, NY 10011
(800) 874-3320

Design: John J.H. Kim
Cover Illustration: Nan Golub

Library of Congress Cataloging-in-Publication Data

Acierno, Maria, 1963-
The children of flight Pedro Pan / by Maria Acierno. -- 1st ed.
p. cm. -- (Stories of the states)
Summary: In Miami in 1961, having just arrived from Cuba
without their parents, ten-year-old Maria and her younger
brother face an uncertain future.
ISBN 1-881889-52-1 : $12.95
[1. Cuban Americans--Fiction. 2. Miami (Fla.)--Fiction.]
I. Title. II. Series.
PZ7.A179Ch 1994
[Fic]--dc20
93-47651

10 9 8 7 6 5 4 3 2 1

Printed in the USA

 # TABLE OF CONTENTS

CHAPTER ONE
There's a Lot I'll Be Learning

"**M**ARIA, GET AWAY FROM THERE BEFORE YOU breathe in too much smoke," Mami said.

Ten-year-old Maria lingered for a moment on the balcony of their large, sprawling, Spanish-tiled home, admiring the rows of *caña*—sugarcane—swaying in the wind. From the terrace of her second-floor bedroom, she could see the acres of stalks neatly lined up in rows. The workers were burning the weeds, and the pungent smell was a reminder that harvest time—*zafra*—would soon be here. The smoke blended with the red and orange colors of the lowering sun, which seemed to be setting at a lazy pace. Maria thought that it, too, seemed hesitant to leave the majestic *caña*.

Maria turned and looked lovingly at her Mami. Isabel Aleman was the most beautiful woman in Cuba's Province of Camaguey. Her long, black hair was pulled back in an elegant bun, which gave her a regal look. Her smooth skin and milky-white complexion contrasted sharply with her dark, almond-shaped eyes and thick, black eyelashes.

"Mami, why do Jose and I have dark skin when yours is so fair?" asked Maria.

"You and your brother have your Papi's coloring. I think it looks like *cafe con leche*," Señora Aleman said, as she looked at herself in the gilded mirror over her handsome, carved dresser. "But when you and I look into each other's eyes, it is as if we're looking at the same reflection."

Maria knew she had the same intense eyes as her Mami, and the same shiny, straight black hair, too, but she felt the resemblance stopped there. She thought her nose and mouth were too big, her legs unusually long, and her gangly body too clumsy. Her ballet classes helped her awkwardness, but it was horseback riding she loved—especially when she rode her beloved black horse, *Negro*, through the *caña* fields.

"*Por favor*, close the doors, Maria. The smoke is too strong today," Mami said.

Maria did as she was told. "*Zafra* will soon be here. I can't wait to help the workers. Am I old enough now to cut the *caña*?" Maria asked, skipping around the spacious, ornately decorated room.

"Come sit next to me, Maria. I have something important to discuss with you," Mami said softly, patting the seat next to her. Maria searched her mother's lovely face. It was lined with worry.

"What's wrong, Mami? You seem so sad," Maria asked, sitting next to her on the loveseat.

Her mother took a deep breath. "Over the last two years, you have heard Papi and me talking about the changes in our country since Fidel Castro came to power in 1959. Some of those changes have not been for the better," Mami began. Maria nodded. She had seen many new, disturbing things— men in fatigues who carried large guns, for instance—and she knew there were food shortages. But none of this really affected her, and she wondered why Mami would mention it now.

Mami continued, "Papi and I feel things are too unsettled for you and Jose to stay here. We think that perhaps it would be best if you went to Miami until things quiet down a bit."

"Like a vacation?" Maria asked excitedly.

"*Sí*, something like that. I don't expect this to last long. All Papi and I want is for you and Jose to be happy and, most of all, safe," Mami answered, her voice quavering.

"When will we leave? What shall I take? Where will we stay?" The questions poured out of Maria. Miami! How exciting!

Mami smiled. "Not so fast, Maria. Papi has taken care of all the arrangements with some help from our friends. You and Jose will be staying with Papi's cousin, Ines, in Miami Beach. You will pack the way you usually do when you visit your Aunt Tati in Havana," Mami said.

Suddenly, Maria realized what her mother was saying. "Mami, aren't you and Papi coming? I thought it was a vacation for all of us."

Mami put her arms around Maria and stroked her long black hair. When Maria looked up, she saw tears in Mami's eyes. Her voice was choked with emotion when she said, "*Mi amor*, you and Jose are the most important part of our lives and there is nothing we love more than both of you. But we must stay and take care of our home and our fields. As you just mentioned, the *zafra* season will soon be here, and since Papi's family has owned this plantation for generations, it is our responsibility to see that nothing goes wrong this year."

The Aleman family's reputation as one of the finest sugar planters in Cuba was well known. But Maria was confused. She could understand the importance of staying to tend the harvest. But why was her mother so upset?

• • •

The week passed quickly. Maria spent the days riding her horse, *Negro*, painting, and attending ballet classes. She helped the maids choose the proper clothes to pack for her trip to Miami, and in the afternoons she and Mami would visit the dress shops in town. The fittings were long and boring, but Mami insisted she have the most perfect wardrobe for her trip to America.

Two days before their departure, Maria and her eight-year-old brother, Jose, decided to take a walk through the *caña*. The tall, yellow stalks of sugar were in a field near the house. The maze of rows was enormous and Maria knew they could easily get lost if they didn't know their way around. Though it was nearly dusk, the August sun was still hot and the brown skin of the sugarcane workers glistened with sweat.

Maria smiled and waved to the men and women as she passed them. Most of the workers had been with them for years. They were like a family. Papi often said that they all depended on each other to make sure the sugar was produced successfully.

As they walked, Jose bent down and picked up a stalk of *caña* and began to chew and suck on it loudly. Maria looked at him and tried to sound like her mother. "Jose, you sound like a *cerdo*. What will Cousin Ines think?"

Jose spit out the stalk. "Pigs are very smart animals. Papi told me so. Anyway, it doesn't matter what Ines thinks because I'm not going to Miami."

Maria stopped walking. This had to be another of Jose's games. "And why not?" she asked patiently.

"Don't you realize *pelota* starts next week? If I'm not there my team will have no one to play first base!" Jose said.

"I'm sure they'll manage," Maria said. "Besides, we won't be gone that long, *hermanito*." Maybe if she could convince Jose, she could convince herself, too.

"Maria, I'm scared," Jose said, his voice growing quiet. "I don't want to leave Camaguey without Mami and Papi."

Maria put her arm around her little brother and took a deep breath. "Don't be scared, Jose. I'll be there and I promise I won't let anything happen to you. You can bring your *pelota* things to Miami and I'll play with you."

Jose laughed. "You hate baseball. And you don't know how to throw."

"Well, I guess there's a lot I'll be learning in Miami," Maria said with a smile. She handed Jose another stalk of *caña* and they both began to chomp like *cerdos* as they walked along the fields.

CHAPTER TWO
Don't Look Back

THE CAR RIDE TO THE AIRPORT IN RANCHO Boyeros was unusually quiet. Mami didn't even seem to notice her favorite rumba songs on the radio. Jose stared out the window in silence. Maria's tall, handsome Papi was usually full of laughter, and he loved to tease the children. But even he seemed to be far away. Periodically, Mami turned around and looked at her children. She didn't say anything. She just gazed at them and seemed to be memorizing their faces.

As the sun was setting, they arrived at the small airport. Waiting for them near the baggage area was their favorite aunt, Mami's older sister, Tia [Aunt] Tati. Jose and Maria ran to her open arms and she squeezed them tightly. Then she reached into her large, brightly colored bag to hand out presents. Jose ripped open his box to find a new leather mitt and baseball. "*Gracias.* I promise to use them every day," Jose said happily.

Maria carefully opened her box and found a paint set, a pad of thick white paper, and a bright red jump rope. "The paint set is for you to capture the beauty of Miami, and the jump rope is to help you teach your new American friends all the fancy steps you know," Tia Tati said.

"*Gracias*, Tia Tati. When I return you will be the first person to see my paintings," Maria replied. Tia Tati turned away quickly.

Mami and Papi were busy with the luggage, speaking to men in dark business suits. BANG! Maria jumped in surprise at the loud sound, but her mother and father didn't seem the least bit startled. "What was that?" she asked.

"Nothing, *mi amor*, just the sound of the plane starting its engine," Mami answered. "Don't worry, children, it's all very safe. After all, this is 1961—these are modern times."

"It's a perfect night for an adventure," Papi added. Although he tried to sound cheerful, his voice seemed different to Maria.

Jose stood transfixed at the big window. Maria joined him and could see there was just as much activity outside as inside the terminal. Men in coveralls were motioning with their hands, luggage was being loaded into the belly of a big plane, and little carts were being pushed around with great care. Jose turned to his father. "Papi, why do those men have *pistolas*?"

Mami and Papi exchanged nervous looks. "It's nothing, Jose. It's only for protection against bandits."

Inside the terminal, there were dozens of people rushing around, trying to hold on to their belongings. Children were dragged along by the hand as parents desperately searched for their gates. People were yelling and shoving. The adults' faces were lined with worry. Most of the children were wide-eyed and open-mouthed.

Maria frantically tried to keep up with her parents and Tia Tati, who were rushing through the terminal. Papi ran ahead, and Maria caught up to her mother. "Where's Papi going?" Maria asked.

"He went to talk to Father Pablo. He'll be right back," Mami explained.

"Why is Father Pablo here?" Jose asked from behind. Maria also thought it was strange that the priest from their church would be here. Perhaps, since he was a close friend of the family, he just wanted to say good-bye.

"He is one of the people who helped us get you on this flight," Mami said.

As they headed out of the main terminal,

Mami suddenly came to a halt. Maria looked up to see a *soldado*. He stood very straight in his green fatigues and he carried a large rifle. "Where are you going? Let me see your papers!" he ordered gruffly.

Tia Tati's face turned pale. She looked at Maria's mother with round, frightened eyes and waited for her younger sister to respond. Mami looked the soldier in the eye. "Excuse us, but my son feels ill. I must get him to the bathroom," she said firmly. The young *soldado* looked at Jose, who clutched his stomach and began to groan loudly.

"Well, hurry. We don't want him getting sick all over the floor," the *soldado* commanded, wrinkling his nose. He stepped aside and let them pass.

As they walked away, Maria noticed that Mami was trembling. Maria's heart was beating fast. She was scared and confused. Why had Mami lied to the soldier?

Finally, they reached Papi. They were at the end of the terminal, which was dark and deserted. "What took you so long?" he asked worriedly.

"A *soldado* stopped us. I pretended to be sick so he'd let us pass," Jose excitedly explained.

Before Jose could demonstrate, Papi interrupted him. In a choked voice he said, "It's time to say good-bye, *hijo*." He knelt and hugged Jose tightly, looking him in the eye. "Be brave and strong. Do what you can to help Cousin Ines, and remember, we love you."

Standing, he turned and looked at his daughter. "Maria, you may not understand everything that is going on, but remember that your Mami and I only want the best for both of you. You will be safe with Ines. She is looking forward to having you with her. Be patient and strong and I promise you, we will be together again." With tears in his eyes, he held her to him and gently kissed her face. Maria could see that her mother was quietly crying.

Maria was doing her best to be brave. But she couldn't swallow the lump in her throat. Her father's solemn words had frightened her. She didn't want to go away without her parents.

Father Pablo came over to them. "We can't hold the plane any longer," he said quietly. "They are getting suspicious." Mami quickly hugged Jose and kissed his face while Tia Tati held Maria.

Then Mami whispered to Maria, "You must look after Jose, for he is still such a child. You have each other for comfort. *Mi amor*, when you start to miss me, look in the mirror and remember that I am always with you." Maria and Mami hugged each other, both with tears running down their cheeks.

"Remember, Maria, paint pictures of everything for us," Tia Tati said, quickly hugging her.

Father Pablo took Maria and Jose by the hand and rapidly walked toward an unmarked door.

As they reached the door, Maria twisted around for one last look at her parents. Father Pablo gently pulled her back. "No, *niña*—only look ahead. Everything will be fine." They walked quickly across the tarmac to the stairs that led to the plane. The priest went up to a tall woman with very blond hair. Then he made the sign of the cross in front of Maria and Jose. "Do not be frightened. All of you on this plane are blessed. You are the lucky ones. You are the *Pedro Pan* children."

As they got to the top of the stairs, the large, heavy airplane door closed behind Maria and Jose. The blond woman took them to their seats. Maria looked around the small, crowded plane. The first thing she noticed was the smell. The pungent air was filled with the odor of perspiration and soiled diapers. There were only children on the plane. Most of them were crying or looked as if they were about to start. "Jose, don't you think it's strange that there are no grown-ups on the plane?" asked Maria.

"The blond woman is a grown-up, and I'm sure the pilot is, too," Jose answered. Maria was suddenly too tired to argue. "Don't worry, *hermana*, I'm sure Mami and Papi know what they are doing," Jose said, smiling weakly at Maria.

Maria leaned back in her sat and thought of her parents. She looked out the small airplane window, hoping to catch sight of them. All she could see was darkness. Papi was right. She did not understand this sudden trip. She was leaving everything behind, and she was afraid she might never see her home again.

Maria quickly wiped away her tears. *I have to be strong*, she thought. *And I must have hope.*

The plane began to move. Jose and Maria held hands, not knowing what to expect. All of the young passengers became silent. When it gained enough speed, the plane began to lift. Maria's heart jumped and Jose let out a squeal.

As the plane leveled off, Maria began to think about the new things she would encounter in Miami. She wondered what Ines was like, and where she lived. What kind of cars, buildings, and stores would she see in Miami Beach? What would the American children be like? How would she talk to them? Would the English she had learned in school be good enough for her to communicate with Americans?

Then she remembered what Father Pablo had said. They were "the *Pedro Pan* children." Wasn't Peter Pan the character in the story she had read in school? The one who led children to Never-Never Land? What did Father Pablo mean?

Soon Maria and Jose drifted off to sleep as the magical lights of Havana seemed to twinkle good-bye.

CHAPTER THREE
We Must Make Do with What We Have

THE JOLT OF LANDING WOKE MARIA AND JOSE. "Where are we?" Jose asked, stretching his long limbs.

"I think we're in Miami," Maria answered. The blond woman told all the children to line up in the aisle of the plane. Slowly they filed through the door and down the steep steps. Maria held tightly to Jose's hand. She looked around in confusion. The terminal was alive with people. The women were wearing full skirts with open-toed shoes, and the men were not wearing ties or suits. The air was hot and muggy.

Jose looked up at Maria. "I'm tired. Where are we going?"

Maria had no answer. She felt the tears begin to well in her eyes. What were they to do?

Suddenly she spied a short, dark-haired woman holding up a sign that said, "Welcome, Jose and Maria." Pulling Jose, Maria hurried to the woman, who dropped the sign. "*Gracias a Dios* you made it. I was beginning to worry. I've been waiting for almost four hours. I'm Ines," she said, smiling. "I recognized you from photographs, but you've grown so much. Let me take a good look at you." She turned them around and gave each a hug.

"I'm so happy you're here. This is for you, Jose, and for you, Maria," Ines continued, handing each a small box. "Well, go ahead and open them while I get your luggage. We can catch the bus right outside." Maria and Jose began to open their boxes as they followed Ines to the crowded bus outside the terminal.

"Do you like them?" Ines asked anxiously once they had found seats. "I hope you do. I nearly drove the saleslady crazy. What's wrong? You haven't said a word."

Jose looked up. "I love the yo-yo. It's just you haven't stopped talking long enough for me to answer."

"Jose! Where are your manners?" Maria chided him.

Ines laughed. "No, he's right. I guess I'm a little nervous. How about you, Maria, do you like your present?"

"It's beautiful," Maria replied, placing the bright comb in her hair. "*Gracias*, Ines," both children said.

"You're welcome, *niños*. I just wish it could've been more," Ines said. After a fifteen-minute trip, Ines led them off the bus. Maria was tired and hungry and her head was spinning with all of the hurried jostling of getting on and off the plane and bus. "My mother will be waiting for us. She's very excited about seeing you again," Ines said.

Maria looked around the neighborhood. Though it was still dark, she could make out rows of small houses, each one sitting close to the next. The shrubs and palm trees seemed to be planted in sand, and the night air smelled of sea water. It was very different from their plantation in Camaguey.

Ines's mother was waiting for them at the door of the small efficiency apartment, located in a plain, white stucco building. She was a small, old woman with white hair, which was neatly combed back into a bun. Smiling at them, she insisted they call her Abuela—grandmother—though her name was Gloria. Maria immediately liked the jovial surrogate grandmother.

The small efficiency had little space and not much furniture. Maria could see the kitchen, bathroom, bedroom, and living room from the front door. The whole apartment was about the same size as her bedroom in Camaguey. She couldn't imagine two people living in such a small space, let alone four people.

The white walls were bare, and the floor was made of cement and fake marble. In the living room was a sagging brown sofa and an old, orange-flowered armchair. A small card table was crammed into the tiny kitchen, next to a black stove, a small sink, and a short, white refrigerator. None of the chairs around the table matched. The bedroom had two small beds with a short, wobbly table between them. A square brown dresser stood in a corner of the room. Hanging on the wall was a silver-framed picture of Ines with her husband, Miguel.

Ines and Abuela pulled out the sofa bed for the children. Jose watched in amazement. "I've never slept on something like that. This is going to be fun."

Maria and Jose got ready for bed, unlocking the suitcases Mami had so carefully packed for them. Maria was exhausted. She closed her eyes and thought about Mami and Papi. She already missed them. But Ines and Abuela were very nice, and she felt comfortable in the small apartment.

She glanced over to Ines's bedroom. She stared at the eight-by-ten wedding picture. In the background were the many guests that had been invited to the Grand Havana Hotel for the festivities. It reminded her of the times Tia Tati would take her to Havana's most famous boulevard, the Malecon. It was a broad and winding ribbon that ran along the beach. They would stroll along, watching the vendors and tourists, and stop to buy treats of *leche frita*, a white fudge, or flaky *empanadas* stuffed with fish or meat. The memories warmed her heart and she fell asleep dreaming of Cuba.

• • •

The next few days passed quickly for Jose and Maria. At first, they didn't venture out much. They preferred to stay in the tiny backyard, which was shared with the three other efficiency apartments. Jose and Maria were the only children. Maria practiced her jump rope routines or painted under the little citrus tree in the corner of the yard. Jose would play baseball, trying to dodge the clothesline that stretched from one end of the area to the other. Every afternoon they would practice their English. Mami had thoughtfully packed their English books from school in Camaguey, and they tried to speak only English to each other for at least one hour a day.

On their fourth night, Maria approached Ines. "Will you be working late tomorrow?" she asked. Ines worked as a housekeeper at a motel. She had been lucky to find the job a few weeks after arriving in Miami, in the summer of 1960. That was almost a year ago, and though her duties were tiresome, she never complained.

Ines looked up from her ironing. "*Sí.* I will leave a chicken in the refrigerator. Maybe you and Abuela can make some potatoes and carrots to go with it. Do you remember how to work the oven?" Maria nodded. Since Ines worked so much, Maria had become very helpful with the daily chores.

Maria took the pressed clothes from Ines and carefully hung them in the small bedroom closet. She removed Ines's housekeeping uniform and put it on the outside hook so it would be ready for her in the morning.

Maria rejoined Abuela and Ines in the kitchen and asked if there was anything else she could do. Abuela looked up from her sewing. "*Sí,* there is something else. I want you to sit and eat a bowl of *natilla.* If you don't start eating more, your clothes are going to fall right off you!"

Maria tugged at her dress, which already seemed to have gotten much bigger. Then she looked at the sweet custard Abuela placed in front of her. She tried her best to eat it, but for some reason, the food didn't have the same taste as it did in Camaguey.

Ines smiled at Maria. "It took a while for me to get used to the food here. I lost ten pounds when I first arrived." She stopped, a faraway look in her eyes. "I can still can taste the big, orange-tinted egg yolks, and the milk with the sweet cream that forms on top. I can remember taking big spoonfuls and dipping hot Cuban bread in it while . . ."

"Enough," snapped Abuela. "There's no use looking back. We must make do with what we have here."

Ines and Maria exchanged knowing looks. No matter how much Abuela went on about "making do," she still kept a packed suitcase under her bed, ready for her return to Cuba.

"Ines, can we still go to the *playa* tomorrow?" asked Maria. The beach had been one of her favorite places in Cuba.

"I'm sorry, but I have to say no. I won't be back until after sundown and it will be too late," answered Ines. Maria's smile faded, but she said nothing. Lowering her head, she began to walk away.

"Wait," Abuela said. "Ines, I can take the children. I'm almost finished with the last of the embroidery and it would be nice to get out for a while." Abuela did piecework, embroidering sweaters on assignment for a large department store. The messenger from the store delivered the pieces to her at the beginning of the week, and she would be paid for each one that was completed when he came back to pick them up.

"I don't know, Mama. Are you sure you feel up to it?" Ines asked.

"*Sí*, don't worry, I'm fine. Anyway, with Maria's help, I'm sure I can make the four-block walk," Abuela answered, as she rubbed her arthritic leg. "A trip to the *playa* is much too important to miss," she added, looking at Maria. Maria smiled gratefully.

The next day when Maria awoke, Ines was already gone and Jose was eating cereal at the small kitchen table. "Come and eat some cereal with *platanos*," Abuela said to Maria. She sat down on one of the plastic-covered chairs.

Jose was shoveling the cereal into his mouth faster than he could chew and talking between large bites of buttered white toast. Jose didn't seem to mind the change in his diet. "Abuela said we're going to the *playa*, and that she's going to take us to the pier to meet her friend," Jose said to Maria.

After breakfast, Maria and Jose played in the backyard while Abuela finished packing away the sweaters she had worked on. She had to wait for the delivery truck. There were only thirty pieces this time, but Maria knew that Abuela very much wanted to help Ines with the household expenses.

Maria propped her painting book against the citrus tree and studied her new creation. Jose threw his baseball in the air and caught it behind his back.

"Out!" he shouted, as the ball landed in his mitt.

Maria jumped in surprise. "Jose, please, I'm trying to concentrate."

"Maria, why do you keep painting pictures of things in Cuba? Tia Tati said to paint scenes of Miami," Jose said.

She shrugged. "I don't know. Every time I start, I think it'll be about Miami, but it turns out to be some place in Camaguey." Maria looked at the latest picture, of her riding *Negro* through the *caña* fields. She was painting better than ever and she didn't understand why it was so difficult to paint the things she saw in Miami.

Finally, around two o'clock, Abuela said it was time to go. They packed towels, a thermos of lemonade, and some peanut butter sandwiches for Jose. Maria took a *platano* for herself and Abuela brought along some saltine crackers. When they reached the beach they saw it was nearly empty since it was a weekday and not in the most popular part of town. "How nice," said Abuela. "We have the *playa* all to ourselves."

Maria stared at the waves rolling in and the white mounds of sand. She took a deep breath of the salty air. Jose ran to the water and jumped in. The seagulls scattered and squawked at the disturbance. Abuela joined Jose and laughed at his antics. "Look, I'm a seagull!" Jose said, as he flapped his arms and mimicked the birds. Maria laughed at her younger brother. Her heart suddenly felt lighter than it had in weeks.

Jose had insisted Maria take her paint book to the beach. He told her she might be "inspired" to paint, especially since she liked the beach so much. Maria opened the book to a blank page and began to paint Jose and Abuela in the blue Atlantic Ocean. But before long the water began to resemble the aqua color of the Caribbean Sea, near her hometown. It was hopeless. She closed the book and decided to join Jose and Abuela in their play.

After they had eaten their snacks, Abuela took the children to the pier. They saw fishermen with tackle boxes, rods and reels, and bait—live and dead. They strolled down the wooden pier, looking from side to side to see what kind of fish the fishermen were bringing in. Near the end of the pier, Abuela took Maria's arm. "I want you to meet my friend," she said in accented English.

At the same moment, a tall man wearing a fishing cap turned around. He had a white beard and mustache and very tanned and wrinkled skin. When he lifted his fishing cap, Maria saw he was almost bald.

"The name is Captain John Nichols. But everyone calls me Captain John. I take it you're Maria, and this must be Jose," he said. "Ever gone fishing?" he asked.

A smile lit up Maria's face and she nodded excitedly. "But only *jojo* fishing," she added.

The old man looked surprised. "Well, that's a new one for me. How do you do that?" he asked.

Maria explained in halting English, "You take a tin can and wrap some line around it. Then you put a hook at the end of the line and throw the line into the water, hanging onto the can."

Captain John shook his head in amazement. "Maybe some day I'll try it," he said. "Will you show me?" Maria nodded shyly.

Abuela said they were just heading back home, but she promised to try to return soon. Captain John reached into his wicker fishing basket and pulled out a four-pound red snapper. "It isn't much, but take it. I hope you all enjoy it," he said.

"*Gracias,*" Abuela said. "Good-bye."

"*Adios,* and my best to Ines," he replied.

Abuela and Maria walked down the pier and caught up with Jose, who had run ahead. "If you ever need anything, go to Captain John," Abuela said. "He's a good man. He retired from the United States Navy years ago. Ines and I met him and his family at church."

Maria turned and waved at her first American friend. Captain John smiled, touching the tip of his cap.

CHAPTER FOUR
I Want to Go Home!

MARIA HAD ALWAYS BEEN A QUICK LEARNER. Back at Camaguey, at her all-girls parochial school, she was the first one to learn her English lessons. During *zafra*, with the help from the workers, she knew exactly how to stack the sugarcane so it could be processed in the large mills. But nothing could have prepared her for the challenge of housework! At home her family had servants to do everything. But this was Miami, not Cuba.

Ines sometimes worked twelve hours a day and would come home exhausted. Maria wanted to do what she could to help Ines and Abuela. Since their stay was only temporary, she felt it was the least she could do for her surrogate family.

Ines first taught Maria how to use the stove. She helped Maria label the knobs on the stove and gave her several safety rules. Maria was soon able to cook rice, vegetables, and even the camomile tea mixture that Abuela and Ines liked.

Jose, on the other hand, only cared about eating the food, not how to prepare it. But he helped in other ways. Maria convinced him that dusting and sweeping up would be useful for his hand-eye coordination. "Jose, Mickey Mantle dusts all the time, and he's one of the greatest players in the game," Maria said, hiding a smile.

Laundry days were always difficult. On Ines's days off, Jose and Maria would help her carry the dirty clothes to the laundromat. It was only three blocks up on Collins Avenue, so they would wrap the clothes inside the bed sheets and walk. The laundromat was in a run-down building. The paint was peeling from the greenish walls and it was only slightly bigger than their apartment. But the smell of fresh detergent, the friendly chatter in Spanish and English, and even the outdated magazines helped make the time pass quickly. The machines were old and overused, but to Maria and Jose, they were modern American appliances. In Camaguey, everyone still used washtubs to clean their clothes.

The difficult part was bringing the wet and heavy clothes back to the house so they could be hung outside with wooden clothespins on the clothesline. In the evening, they would bring in the laundry and fold it so it could be put away. It was hard work but Maria took pride in the chore, since it was the first time she had ever been responsible for her clothes. When it was completed, Ines would give them warm milk and sponge cake, which was a favorite with Jose. "For this I would do laundry every day . . . well, almost every day," Jose would say, as he dunked a piece of cake in his milk.

Maria enjoyed going on errands with Ines since it gave her the chance to see different areas in Miami. As they rode the bus early in the morning while Jose played in the backyard at home, Maria would watch as residential neighborhoods changed into business areas. There were office buildings, clothing stores, restaurants, and an array of shops that displayed books, jewelry, and "45s"—small vinyl records. Ines called the area "Downtown." Maria liked Downtown. The busy streets reminded her of Camaguey's business section.

Their first stop was the Bank of Miami. Maria loved the feel of the thick, plush carpet beneath her feet as she walked into the lobby. The cool air that rushed out of the air-conditioning units in the windows was a welcome relief from the hot, muggy air outside.

Ines would deposit half of Abuela's earnings from her piecework. She explained to Maria how important the weekly transaction was to them. "We save the money because you never know what will happen. We never expected to be here, in this position, but we are and we need to always keep an eye on the future." Maria solemnly agreed.

Next, they would either walk the two blocks to the pharmacy or they would get back on the bus to travel the two miles, past the strip of shops and restaurants, to the Five and Dime store.

The first time they went to the pharmacy, Maria was struck by the smell. The lotions, medicines, and tonics gave off a strong, clean odor. Ines talked in Spanish with the man behind the counter as he prepared Abuela's medicine for her leg. Before leaving, Maria would be given a lollipop from the glass jar next to the cash register. One day, Ines told Maria, "Dr. Garcia came from Havana two years ago. He was a very important heart surgeon there."

"Why isn't he working in a hospital?" Maria asked.

"Because he doesn't have an American medical license. But he studies at night and hopes that one day he can resume his practice here," Ines replied.

Maria was impressed with Dr. Garcia's determination, but wondered why he would want to stay in Miami. "Ines, when will Dr. Garcia return to Havana?" she asked.

Ines hesitated and then said sadly, "I don't

think that will ever happen."

"But why?" Maria asked in surprise. Ines looked around nervously and seemed relieved when the bus came. She changed the subject and Maria never got an answer.

The Five and Dime was one of Maria's favorite places. The store was filled with colorful displays of inexpensive trinkets, cosmetics, and household items. Here they would buy Abuela's embroidery needles, cleaning supplies, shampoo, talcum powder, and soap. Maria loved to look at the large selection of American products, picking out things she would like to own. She would finger the satin ribbons and choose the red ones to match the beads that would go around her long neck. Then she would go to the makeup counter and try to decide which shade of lipstick would look best with her ensemble. It was a fun game, but of course it was only pretend.

Usually, they would stop at the lunch counter to sit and drink thick, chocolate milk shakes. During these trips, Maria would be reminded of her visits with Tia Tati in Havana. There they would go to the lunch counter at F.W. Woolworth's and eat Cuban sandwiches, grilled Cuban bread filled with sweet ham, spiced pork, Swiss cheese, and pickles. Then they would wash it down with *guarapo*, made from sugarcane juice, or shakes made from tropical fruits like mango or coconut. "Ines, the *bâtidos* in Cuba are delicious, but I think these chocolate shakes here are my favorite," Maria would say.

If Ines had any extra coins she would buy Jose and Maria some penny candy. During one trip, as they were leaving the store, Maria spotted a small transistor radio for sale. She couldn't take her eyes off it. "Isn't it beautiful?" she breathed.

Ines looked at the price tag and smiled regretfully. "Yes, it's very nice. Maybe one day we could get one." They walked out quietly, each lost in her own little dream.

Sunday was the day reserved for worship. They always attended the 9:30 morning mass at St. Rose of Lima. They would dress in their best clothes and take the Sixth Avenue bus to Miami Shores, where the church was located. Once there, Ines would light a candle for her husband, Miguel, who was still in Cuba, and then they would kneel at the altar with their rosary beads, and recite the Lord's Prayer. The mass was conducted by Father Paul in Latin, and the hymns were sung in English. The organ accompanied the choir, and Maria sang along softly in Spanish.

On the third Sunday after their arrival, Maria and Jose were leaving the church with Ines and Abuela when Father Paul asked them to stay and join him for refreshments. He was a kind, elderly man who spoke softly, and he had been very helpful to Ines and Abuela when they first arrived in Miami. Father Paul had found the job at the motel for Ines and let her and Abuela stay at the nuns' quarters until they found the efficiency apartment.

They sat in Father Paul's living room and his assistant, John, brought them coffee and cold sodas in tall glass bottles. He asked the children how they were getting along. Jose replied between gulps of soda, "Fine, but it's so hot!"

"Yes, it's true, Miami is very hot and humid. But your home in Cuba was hot, too, wasn't it?"

Jose nodded. Then Father Paul said, "Why don't you and Maria go ask John if there are any butter cookies left?"

Maria and Jose didn't find John, but they did find two butter cookies on the kitchen counter. When they came back into the living room with their *bizcochos*, they saw Abuela drying her eyes and Ines hugging Father Paul. Maria stood frozen. Something was wrong, but she was too scared to ask what was happening.

Father Paul saw the children and smiled weakly, but his troubled eyes were anything but happy. "So are the cookies good?" he asked.

Maria nodded woodenly and thanked him as Ines and Abuela gathered their purses to leave. A few minutes later they said their good-byes and

John drove them home.

No one spoke for a long time, and Abuela stayed in the kitchen preparing lunch. Maria and Jose changed clothes and sat quietly on the sofa. After what seemed like an eternity, Ines called them into the bedroom.

"*Niños*, we need to talk," Ines began. "Father Paul gave me a letter from your parents. They are fine, but the situation in Cuba has gotten worse. Your parents have decided it would be best if they left Cuba and came here."

Jose yelped with glee, but Maria remained silent, frozen in her spot.

"Since you will be staying, we need to enroll you in school," Ines continued. "You'll attend Miami Beach Elementary School, which is only three blocks away from here. I'll take you there tomorrow, and afterward we'll take a walk to the beach." Ines tried to sound enthusiastic, but when she looked into Maria's eyes, Maria knew Ines wasn't telling them everything.

But Jose was bursting with excitement. "When are Mami and Papi coming?" he asked.

Ines said, "I don't know. Father Pablo will be helping them just as he helped you, and he will let us know when it will happen. Be patient, Jose. I know it will be hard, but you must stay strong." Jose nodded happily and rushed to the kitchen to tell Abuela.

"Maria, what's wrong? I thought you would be happy," Ines said.

Maria bit her lip and blinked back tears. "Ines, of course I'm glad I'll be seeing my parents, but I thought I'd be seeing them in Cuba, not here," she said, her voice shaking.

Ines closed the bedroom door and faced Maria. "*Niña*, calm down, please. We don't want to upset Jose. I realize this is difficult but Fidel Castro's regime has made it impossible for people like your parents to remain in Cuba. Since they oppose the current government, they are in serious danger. They have to leave, Maria. It's the only way, and it's for the best," Ines said.

"But my life is in Camaguey. I don't want to go to school here. I want to go home!" Maria burst out in a flurry of sobs and tears.

Ines wrapped her arms around Maria and held her for a long time. Rocking her back and forth, Ines repeated, "*No mires para atras*—Don't look back."

"How can I not look back?" Maria sniffled, her face pressed against Ines's dress. Her heart felt like a rock in her chest. "What will happen to *Negro* and my toys and my clothes? What will happen to our house? Will I never see my friends and Tia Tati again? Everything is gone!"

CHAPTER FIVE
One Smart Cookie

IN THE DAYS AND WEEKS THAT FOLLOWED INES'S announcement, Maria's life was again turned upside-down. When she had thought her stay in Miami was temporary, she had wanted to help Ines and Abuela. But now that she knew she would be here permanently, all she wanted was to return to Cuba. She didn't want to paint anymore, and though she still helped to cook, it wasn't with the same enthusiasm.

Maria was angry, too. She was angry with Fidel Castro, of course, and even with her parents and Abuela and Ines. She felt that everyone had lied to her.

She still went to the beach with Ines and Jose, but mostly because she didn't want to hear her little brother whine and beg her to join them. Ines allowed Maria to go to the pier while she and Jose played in the sand. Maria would sit at the end of the pier and look out toward the horizon. She would wonder what Mami was doing and what kind of day it was in Camaguey. Then she would hear her name being called, as if from across the ocean. But it would only be Jose or Ines. Maria would turn and say good-bye to Captain John, who was always fishing at the pier, and walk away.

One day, Captain John approached her. "I've seen you sitting in the same spot, with the same look on your face, for over a week. Don't you like to play on the beach?" he asked.

Maria sighed. She didn't feel like talking right now. But she couldn't be rude to Abuela's friend. She shook her head no.

"Well, I know you like to fish, so why don't you help me out?" Captain John said.

Before she could say, "No, thank you," the old man had handed her a hook and asked her to bait it. Maria easily slipped the wiggly shrimp on the hook. Captain John nodded his approval. When he asked her to reel in one of the lines, she told him she didn't know how.

"But if you can bait a hook, you must know how to reel in a line," Captain John said.

"Remember, I only know how to *jojo* fish," Maria said. "Papi and I would go to the pier every

Saturday morning and spend the day fishing." She looked back into the water sadly.

"Why don't you teach me?" Captain John said. "I need a new trick and you promised to show me yours. These fish are getting smart and I haven't been able to catch anything decent."

Maria had to smile. She knew Captain John was only trying to cheer her up. He never had any trouble catching fish. Still, she was curious to see if her method of fishing could outsmart the underwater creatures on these shores.

She found an old metal can on the pier and quickly wound some line around it, using it as a rod. Jerking her arm up expertly, she twirled several feet of line and a hook overhead in a circle and flung the line out to sea.

Captain John raised his eyebrows in surprise. "That's definitely a new one for me," he said. After a couple of minutes, Maria pulled up her line. Attached to the end was a good-sized snapper. Maria glowed with delight. "A *pargo*! I knew it would work!"

Captain John helped her remove the fish from the hook. "How did your dad learn about this yo-yo?" he asked.

Maria smiled. "It's not like the toy 'yo-yo.' In Spanish it's spelled with a 'j' but it's pronounced the same. It was used by the Tainos Indians on the island. Papi's ancestors were Tainos and he always taught Jose and me the old customs."

"Well, now I'll teach you something new," Captain John said. "Then you can teach your dad how to use a rod and reel."

Maria watched as Captain John showed her how to hold the fishing rod and cast the line into the water. On her first try, Maria flung the line into the water in one smooth motion. She smiled and settled in to wait for a catch while Captain John practiced with the *jojo* line.

"Abuela told me you'll be starting school next week," Captain John said.

Maria nodded. "Jose and I will be going to Miami Beach Elementary."

"That's the same school my granddaughter, Denise, goes to," Captain John said. "What grade will you be in?"

"I should be going into the fifth grade, but I have to take a test first to see if I'm smart enough," Maria said, watching her line carefully.

"Don't you worry. Anyone who can catch a fish like you is definitely one smart cookie," Captain John said.

Maria laughed at the funny expression. Then she asked, "Where's Denise now?"

"She's at home," Captain John said. "She and her mother live with me because her dad drives a truck and is away a lot. She's got two younger brothers, too. You and Denise would like each other. She's going to be in the fifth grade, too."

Maria heard her name being called. Ines was waving at her from the beach. She handed the fishing rod to Captain John and thanked him politely for the lesson. He wrapped her fish in some newspaper and said, "Come back tomorrow and I'll bring Denise along so you can meet her."

Maria yelled, "Okay!" as she ran down the pier to show Ines and Jose her *pargo*.

The next day, Maria spent the whole afternoon at the beach with Denise. Maria thought Denise looked like Cinderella. She had long blond hair, clear blue eyes, and her freckled skin was as fair as baby powder. But when Maria told Denise she looked like Cinderella, Denise laughed. "Well, if that's true, then you look like an exotic princess." Now Maria had to laugh.

Maria soon found out that Denise knew almost every inch of the beach. "I practically grew up here," Denise said. "I used to come every day to fish with Grandpa. That was when I was younger. Now I like to have people come to my house, or go to theirs.

"Oh," she said, pausing. "There's one thing you should know about me. Everyone says I talk too much. I don't think it's true, but that's what they say. Especially my younger brothers, who remind me all the time. Anyway, you can interrupt me any time. Everyone does." A wide grin spread across her freckled face.

Maria smiled. "Ines says I'm too quiet. So I guess we'll be a good match. Only please don't talk too fast. I'm still learning English."

Maria found out that Denise loved to jump rope and, as Maria did in Camaguey, took ballet lessons. And she learned that Denise didn't see her father much because of his work.

At first, Maria felt a pang of sadness as Denise talked about how much she missed her father. Maria knew only too well what that felt like. But as Denise talked on, Maria began to feel better. Here, finally, was someone who knew how she felt.

"Are you excited about starting school? It's a great place. I've been going there all my life," Denise said.

"Well, I'm kind of *nervosa*...nervous," Maria admitted. "I'm not sure what grade I'm in, and I don't know anybody."

"You know me, and I'll introduce you to all my friends. You'll see—everyone's really nice, and I'm sure you'll like it," Denise said. "And I know they'll like you. You're pretty and smart and nice," Denise said, counting off on her fingers.

"I hope they like me," Maria said. Denise

squeezed her hand and smiled.

When the first day of school arrived, Maria's stomach was in knots. Jose was excited as he sat eating his breakfast, but Maria couldn't eat a thing. Jose chattered away as they walked with Ines the few blocks to the school, but Maria clutched her notebook, pencil box, and jump rope tightly.

She had passed the school test with flying colors. She would be in the fifth grade, and Jose would be in third. But passing hadn't helped her nerves. She wished her mother could be here, to hold her hand like she had back in Camaguey.

When they reached the long, one-story building, Maria helped Jose find his classroom. When he said good-bye she could hear the small catch in his voice. "Don't worry, *hermanito*. Just talk about baseball and you'll be fine," she told him. He grinned broadly and turned away.

Maria found her own class and walked through the doorway with her heart thumping. Instantly, she felt her face turn red. She looked so different from everyone else. She had on a simple plaid cotton dress and sandals, but the other girls wore crisp shirtwaist dresses with full skirts and ballerina slippers with neat white socks. Most of them wore their hair in bouncy ponytails, while her straight black hair hung loose with a small barrette on the side.

Maria quickly found her seat and slouched down, wishing she could become invisible. For the rest of the morning, the only time she lifted her eyes from her desk was to look for Denise and give her a small smile. It was difficult to understand her teacher, who spoke English so quickly, and Maria felt self-conscious about her accent when she was asked to say her name.

Denise caught up with her as they filed out of the classroom at noon. Together they walked to the noisy lunchroom. Maria's head hurt and her nervousness had made her tired.

"How was your first morning?" Denise asked, showing her how to get the lunch tray and leading her down the line in front of the food displayed in open cases. Women in hairnets and white uniforms stood behind the cases, serving the food.

"There are so many things to learn," Maria said. She looked up as a woman dropped a pasty glob on her plate and covered it with thick, brown liquid. Next came leafy green balls.

"Brussels sprouts," explained Denise. "They're disgusting."

Maria shook her head and gulped.

She sat with Denise at a nearby table and tried to figure out what was on her tray that she could eat. The only things she recognized were white bread and cherry Jell-O, which, along with chocolate cake and milk, became her lunch. Still, at least she had a friend to sit with.

Next came recess. Denise introduced Maria to five of her friends. Maria nodded shyly at them. The girls began an animated discussion about which game they should play. Maria watched quietly until Denise said, "Let's jump rope." Then Maria's eyes lit up. She waited for her turn, carefully turning the rope for the other girls. When she finally jumped in, she did her best routine, one she had mastered with the red jump rope Tia Tati gave her. She didn't make one mistake. The girls cheered and begged Maria to teach them how she did it. Maria happily went through the routine again.

By afternoon, Maria was a little more relaxed. She had actually begun to look around the room. The class practiced the multiplication tables together, so her accent, which she was so worried about, was barely noticeable. And she already knew the multiplication tables. Her teacher, Mrs. Jeffries, complimented her on her ability.

Abuela picked them up after school. Jose wanted to tell them everything about the day, especially about his baseball game at recess. Abuela finally turned to Maria. "And you?"

Maria smiled. "It wasn't so bad." And she had to admit, it really hadn't been. Maybe Miami wouldn't be so bad, she thought to herself.

CHAPTER SIX
It's Time to Tell Them Everything

"JOSE, YOU'RE GOING TO FALL," ABUELA warned. "I won't fall," Jose said impatiently. "You'll see—once I'm done, it'll look perfect."

From the kitchen, Maria overheard Jose and Abuela arguing about where to place the Christmas wreath. She continued to peel the turnips and hum Christmas carols. "That boy is going to give Abuela a heart attack," Ines said, chuckling. Maria looked up with concern.

"No, *niña*, I'm only kidding. Abuela's heart is very sound. It's her leg we need to worry about," Ines said.

Maria nodded and whispered, "The cane you bought for her Christmas gift will help a lot."

"Shh, her hearing is perfect. But you're right. It will be very useful for her walks. I just hope she'll use it. You know how *terca* she can be," Ines whispered back.

"Who's stubborn?" Abuela asked, limping into the kitchen.

Ines and Maria looked at each other, smiling. "Everything looks so beautiful, Abuela. You did a wonderful job for *Nochebuena*," Maria said.

Maria could hardly believe Christmas was here already. She had been so involved with school that the months had flown by. Slowly, she had begun to accept the fact that Miami would be her new home. As difficult as it was to accept, at least she would soon be with her parents again.

Jose and Maria had participated in their first Halloween. Abuela had made their costumes. Maria had dressed up like a princess and Jose, of course, as a baseball player. They had bobbed for apples with Denise and her brothers. That had been Maria's favorite part. Jose, naturally, loved the abundance of candy corn, chocolate bars, and lollipops that he had received trick-or-treating. It was the first time since arriving in America that Maria and Jose agreed they were glad to be in Miami.

The aroma from the kitchen was intoxicating. Ines had been able to find a leg of pork for the traditional Christmas Eve dinner. Ines basted the *lechon* in the oven. "It was definitely a stroke of *buena suerte* when I found the pig farm," she said.

But Maria knew that good luck had had little to do with it. Ines had worked double shifts at the motel for two weeks to earn extra money. Then she had traveled sixty miles on a bus to the town of Homestead and pleaded with a farmer to sell her the prime cut of meat. She wanted her small family to be able to have a traditional *Nochebuena* meal.

Jose tried to sneak a taste from the platter, which was arranged with figs and dates, but Abuela pulled it out of his reach. "*Niño*, you could eat all day if we let you. Here, have one, but no more because you need to save room for dinner."

Maria smiled and remembered how Jose and Mami had had the same conversation last Christmas Eve. The house had been filled with relatives and friends. The music and chattering was festive and everyone was happy. In Camaguey, they would roast a whole pig, seasoned with garlic, lime juice, sour oranges, and spices. It would be placed on hot coals and covered with palm leaves. Maria wondered what her parents were doing this *Nochebuena*, and began to feel the heavy weight on her heart.

As Abuela, Jose, Ines, and Maria gathered around the table, they admired the feast. Abuela placed a small holiday plant in the center. It had a plastic figure of Santa Claus holding out a present. Maria still couldn't get used to seeing the figure of Santa Claus everywhere. In Cuba, she and Jose waited for the arrival of the Three Kings on January Sixth. Instead of writing to Santa, they had written to the Three Kings to ask for gifts.

But in honor of their new homeland, Jose and Maria had agreed to celebrate "American style." Abuela turned out the lights and they all admired the twinkling Christmas tree, which Captain John, Denise, and her brothers had brought over the night before, covered with left-over decorations. As Ines said the blessing, Maria looked around and suddenly felt grateful. Even though Mami and Papi couldn't be there, she knew she was with family.

They waited until midnight to exchange gifts. Abuela opened up her present first and took out the mahogany cane. At first she hesitated, but then relaxed into a smile. "I feel like a grand lady, and it is beautiful. *Gracias*, Ines. *Gracias, niños.*"

The children gave Ines her present. As she opened the box and looked inside, tears sprang to her eyes. It was a miniature nativity scene. "Do you like it?" Jose asked. "Abuela found the manger, and Maria and I made the figures out of corn husks and pipe cleaners Captain John gave us."

Ines was so overwhelmed that she couldn't speak for a moment. She just kept shaking her head. Then she said, "This is the best present I could ask for. Help me place the *nacimiento* under the tree."

They looked at the nativity scene with its lopsided angels, the animals that all looked the same, and the wise men that had to be propped up. They decided it was the nicest *nacimiento* they'd ever seen.

Then Ines went into her bedroom and emerged with a box for Jose and Maria. They carefully opened it as Abuela and Ines looked on. When they saw the gleaming, silver-colored radio, Jose's eyes grew wide and Maria gasped. "Wow! Does it really work?" Jose asked.

"Well, not if you leave it in the box," Abuela said, laughing. "Take it out and plug it in."

Jose hurried to find an outlet. Ines fiddled with the buttons on the radio, and suddenly the sounds of Christmas music filled the room. Everyone cheered and hugged. That night they fell asleep as music played softly in the background.

The holidays passed quickly. They celebrated New Year's Eve with the tradition of eating twelve grapes, one for each month, as the clock struck midnight. The next day was a frenzy of cleaning. Abuela and Ines ceremoniously emptied out the buckets of dirty water as they filled. "Now the house is cleansed of all the bad luck and troubles from the old year," Ines announced. "Nineteen sixty-two will be a year filled with good luck."

When Maria and Jose returned to school, they were eager to see how their new friends had spent their vacation. Maria's class had grown in size. As she scanned the faces of the new students, her mouth fell open in astonishment. One of the new students was her friend Vilma, from her hometown! She could hardly believe it. At lunch, Maria ran over to give Vilma a joyful hug. "When did you get here?" she asked excitedly.

"We were lucky to get out right before Christmas. Things are really bad in Cuba," Vilma said sadly.

Maria had so many questions to ask about Mami and Papi, she hardly knew where to start. Suddenly, she heard yelling and scuffling from the schoolyard. She ran to the windows with the other students.

Then her eyes grew wide. Jose, his clothing torn and his hair in his face, was being marched from the schoolyard by the principal, who looked very angry.

Maria ran to the principal's office. "Go back to your class, Maria. I'll take care of this," Mrs. Dale, the principal, said sternly.

Maria shook her head. There was no way she was going to leave—not with Jose in trouble. Since they had no telephone at home, Mrs. Dale called Ines at work. Maria and Jose sat in silence on a bench in the principal's office, waiting for Ines. Jose stared straight ahead angrily.

Mrs. Dale gave Jose a tissue to clean up. His face was flushed with anger, and even though he wanted to control them, the tears spilled over. He tried to tuck in his shirt, but it was ripped in so many places it was impossible.

Ines arrived in minutes, still wearing her maid's uniform and out of breath. Mrs. Dale faced the three of them. "I understand that what happened today was an ugly act of prejudice," she began. "But to react with violence is unacceptable."

"But they started it!" Jose interrupted. "They called me an orphan. They told me to go back to Cuba, with all the other Negroes," he explained between sniffles. Ines and Maria gasped in shock. How could anyone say such things to Jose? Maria had heard some whispers behind her back, and knew that some of the girls stared at her. But no one had ever said anything to her face.

"I know, Jose. I saw it all, and those boys will be punished. But Jose, you threw the first punch," Mrs. Dale reminded him. "Unfortunately, I doubt this will be the last time you will experience such attitudes. If you don't learn to control yourself, I'm afraid you'll be suspended or expelled. I cannot allow fighting in my school for any reason."

As they left Mrs. Dale's office, Ines prodded Jose and he mumbled an apology to the principal. They walked home in silence. When they arrived,

Abuela was surprised and alarmed. As Jose cleaned up and Ines explained to Abuela what had happened, Maria sat on the sofa, her mind whirling. Why had this happened?

In Camaguey, her friends had never talked about the different colors of their skin. But of course, now they were not in Cuba. They were in America, and to everyone else, they were the outsiders. They didn't belong. They spoke with accents and their skin was darker than that of the other children in the school.

Maria could feel herself getting angry. Why were they working so hard to get used to living in America when they weren't even wanted here? Jose sat down next to her. "Are you all right?" Maria asked him quietly.

"Yeah, I'm fine. I just don't understand why they were so mean. I didn't do anything to them. I was only playing ball," Jose said with a shrug.

Ines and Abuela came in, but Maria barely noticed them. She was so angry she felt her head would burst. Tears brimmed in her eyes. "If they don't want us here then I think we should go back to Cuba," she said firmly. "No matter how bad things are there, at least we'd be home."

Ines turned to Abuela. Then she sighed. "It's time to tell them everything."

CHAPTER SEVEN
You Were the Chosen Ones

MARIA SAT ON THE SAND WITH HER PAINT SET and tried to figure out which color she should use to paint Captain John's fishing cap. It was a warm, sunny day in April, and the humid air had been momentarily pushed aside by the slight breeze of the ocean. The palm trees swayed in the distance.

Maria could see Abuela laughing at Jose as he tried to jump the waves. Maria pulled out the tube of gray paint and searched for her thin paintbrush. Buried deep in the box, she saw the letter that Ines had given her in January. It was from Mami and Papi. She remembered the day clearly, and it was only in the last few weeks that she could think about it without crying.

Maria could still hear Ines's words: "You were

the chosen ones. The *Pedro Pan* children." She had remembered Father Pablo telling them the same thing so many months ago. She hadn't really understood what he meant, but now she knew that they were like the children in the famous story, *Peter Pan*, because they, too, had made a journey without their parents, to a place that would bring them hope for their future.

Maria realized now there was no way they would be returning to Cuba. Ines had told her things in Cuba were very different. Her parents knew that under Fidel Castro they would not have the kind of lives they had led before. Mami had written that there was no free speech, no free thinking—not even the right to believe in what they wanted to. If that was true, then Ines was right. Maria didn't want to return.

It was not until that day that she had learned why Ines's husband, an attorney, stayed in Cuba. She had thought Miguel had stayed to care for his elderly parents. But he had actually stayed to help obtain visa waivers, the special papers needed to travel from one foreign country to the other, for the children who were to escape. Ines had warned the children not to speak about the *Pedro Pan* Operation since many people who were still in Cuba could be jailed for their participation in it.

Maria knew she should feel lucky that she

and Jose had been able to get out when they did. She had asked Ines if Mami and Papi were all right and Ines had nodded solemnly. "They tried very hard to save the sugar mill, but the government took it over. They lost everything, but they were able to get to Havana. Father Paul has learned that they are staying with your relatives there."

Maria had pulled her knees up to her chest, rocking back and forth in a ball. The tears had streamed down her face as she thought of the workers, the rows of sugarcane, and the hard work that had gone into building up the plantation for generations. Now it was all gone. She couldn't believe it!

"Miguel is helping them, and I believe soon all of them will be joining us," Ines had continued. "The connections Miguel made in the past as a lawyer have turned out to be useful."

Abuela, who had been in the bedroom, had joined them. She had been carrying the suitcase that she had kept under her bed since her arrival in America. "*Niños*, it's time we make America our home. Miami is not Camaguey, and it will take time before people accept the changes—but it will happen." And she had handed the suitcase she had finally unpacked to Ines to be put away in storage.

"What are you thinking about? You seem far away." Captain John's voice broke through Maria's memories.

"I was just thinking about everything that has happened in the last few months," Maria answered, putting the letter safely back in its place.

"You've had your ups and downs, I know. But you never know what life is going to bring, and that's what makes it so exciting," the old man said. Maria smiled in agreement and began to paint as he asked, "No fishing today? I think they're biting."

"Not today, Captain John. I feel like painting again, and I want to make sure I put down on paper all the things that are important to me," she replied. "You never know when I'll get a chance to show them off." Maria was thinking of the day she'd be reunited with her parents.

"What are you painting?" he asked, trying to sneak a glance.

Maria put her hand over the paper. "Not till I'm finished. Then I promise I'll show it to you." She smiled. Captain John's portrait was turning out perfectly, Maria thought. She hoped to have it completed by Easter. It was to be her gift to Captain John for his help and friendship.

Maria had just put the finishing touches on Captain John's beard when she heard Jose calling her name. "Well, I guess it's time to go," she said, packing up her belongings. Captain John handed her a newspaper-wrapped fish. "Jose must be excited about the game this weekend. It's the first time the Cougars have made it to the championship."

"Yes, it's very exciting. All he does is practice day and night. Will you be there?" Maria asked.

"I wouldn't miss it for the world," Captain John promised.

Saturday morning they all headed for the nearby baseball park. The stands were filled. It was only nine o'clock but the sun was already beating down hard. Maria waved to Captain John, Denise, and her brothers. They were just settling down on the hard wooden benches when the game began.

By the ninth inning, the score was tied, 1-1, and Jose was up at bat. Abuela yelled out in Spanish, "Hit it as hard as you can and send the ball to Cuba!" Jose looked up and smiled. At the first pitch, he swung at the ball with all his might. It flew over the outfield fence.

Everyone in the Cougars' stands went wild, cheering and shouting. When Jose reached home plate, the whole team greeted him and hoisted him up in the air. The trophy for Most Valuable Player went to Jose, and he beamed with pride as he accepted the honor.

That night, before Jose fell asleep, he turned to Maria. "I can't believe we really won. You know, a few of those guys made fun of me when I first joined the team. But now they want me to practice with them." Maria smiled at her not-so-baby brother and said, "You did great. I'm very proud of you."

Jose stared at the ceiling. "The only thing that would make all this perfect would be if Mami and Papi were here with us," he said a little sadly.

Maria caught her breath and replied, "They are here, Jose—in our hearts. Now go to sleep and dream about the Major Leagues."

Easter came and Maria presented Captain John with her painting of him. The old sailor studied the portrait carefully, in silence. Then he looked up with tears in his eyes. His gravelly voice cracked when he finally said, "Thank you, my dear." Maria knew her painting had been a success.

When school started after the spring break, there were more changes. Almost every day, a loud siren would blast and all the children would have to hide underneath their desks, as they were instructed by Mrs. Jeffries. The teacher explained that it was like a fire drill. In case of any emergency they had to be prepared. But it was scary. The fire drills had only come occasionally; these sirens rang every day. Maria and Jose had asked Ines what it meant. She had simply said, "Don't worry. There's no problem." And Maria tried to believe her.

But it was hard to keep from worrying. Ines had told Maria and Jose that the secret flights of children from Cuba had stopped. She had said it was much too dangerous for children to come by themselves now, and the U.S. government was discouraging travel between the two countries. Maria knew the situation had become very serious.

Still, they tried to go on as normally as possible. As Mother's Day approached, Maria made plans for the traditional festivities. In Cuba, this was a very special holiday. Mothers and daughters would prepare what they would wear months in advance, as it was a tradition for mother and daughter to dress identically when they went to church that Sunday. Children in Cuba would also wear a red or white carnation on Mother's Day to indicate if their mother was alive or dead.

Maria remembered how she and Jose would write a poem for Mami, and she would sit in her favorite chair as they recited it. This year, Jose and Maria made a card for Ines and Abuela. The card thanked them for all they had done to make them feel welcome, safe, and loved. Maria smiled through tears when Abuela taped her card next to her bed.

Ines gave Jose and Maria a red carnation. "*Niños*, I realize this has been a difficult time for you, but you've been very brave. I have a feeling this will be over soon," Ines said. "Your mother would be very proud of you."

Maria beamed as she walked into church wearing her red carnation. She knelt down on the pew and prayed that Ines would be right.

Soon there were only days left until summer vacation. Maria sat impatiently at her desk each day, fidgeting as she waited for the dismissal bell. She was eager to have her days free to go to the beach, paint, or play outside with Jose or her new friends.

One evening, Maria had begun preparing rice on the stove as she waited for Ines to arrive home from work. Jose had just come in from the backyard with his baseball mitt and ball. When she heard Ines come through the front door, Maria turned around with a smile. But when she saw the look on Ines's face, her smile dropped.

Ines sat down on one of the kitchen chairs without taking off her sweater. Her face was pale and her lips were shut together in a tight line.

"What is it, Ines? Are you feeling all right?" Maria asked in a sudden panic.

Ines sighed. "Yes, I'm fine. It's just...well, I got a telephone call from Father Paul today."

Maria's heart sank. *What now?*

Ines looked at Jose and Maria with gentle, sorrowful eyes. "Father Paul got word today that Cuban planes are no longer being allowed to land in the United States. I'm so sorry, *niños*."

Maria stared at Ines. She felt as if everything in her was begin drained away. How could it be? If the planes couldn't land, her parents would never get to the United States. And she would never see Mami and Papi again.

CHAPTER EIGHT
Together, at Last

"Have faith, *niños*," Ines said as she wiped away Jose's and Maria's tears. "I know Miguel will do everything he can to get them out." Ines tried to sound hopeful, but she couldn't lie to them. The future was uncertain for anyone's escape.

For the next few days, Maria felt as she had never felt before. There seemed to be nothing to hope for. She began to listen to the news reports on the radio. All forms of escape, including the airport, the beaches, and the ports, were being monitored closely. Many Cubans had arrived since she and Jose had come that August night in 1961. But now the situation was different. The news reports spoke of a "great threat" that could come from Cuba.

One night Maria ran to Ines's room in tears. She sat down next to Ines on the bed and hugged her. "What is it, *niña?*" Ines asked.

"The man on the radio said Miami might be bombed by Cuba. Is it true? Could that really happen?" Maria asked between sobs.

Ines took a deep breath. "No, it's not possible. I don't want you to get upset. There is tension between Cuba and America, but all the talk about bombs is exaggerated. I promise, you and Jose are safe. Now go to bed."

Maria stopped listening to the news reports. They scared her. And she was never satisfied with the answers she got to her questions. She realized that Ines, Abuela, Captain John, and even Mrs. Jeffries, her teacher, didn't want her to worry. But she felt left out. It was frustrating.

Jose was looking forward to a busy summer vacation, and even Maria began to feel excited when Ines told her of her plans. She had arranged for Maria to attend ballet classes with Vilma and Denise. She would clean the ballet school at night in exchange for free lessons for Maria. Ines had never told Maria about the arrangement, but Maria had overheard her tell Abuela, and she was very grateful. Jose was going to try out for soccer and he was confident he would make the team.

But after school ended, the long summer days began to wear on Maria and Jose. They started to bicker. It always began with something small.

Jose wouldn't help with chores, or Maria would tease Jose about his appetite. Maria realized she was often being unfair, but she couldn't help herself. She just felt that Jose was not helping out.

After one particularly fierce argument, Maria stormed out of the tiny apartment and went to the pier. She found Captain John at his usual spot and sat down next to him.

"What's wrong, Maria? You look mad enough to spit," Captain John said.

She didn't understand why anyone would want to spit out in anger, but agreed with him anyway. "Yes, I'm very angry," she said, spitting.

Captain John tried not to laugh. "What happened?" he asked gently.

"Jose is such a baby. I can't stand taking care of him anymore. All he does is think about playing, not about helping with the chores. Today he refused to put his clothes away. 'I have no time. I have to get to soccer practice. You do it,'" Maria said, mimicking him. "So I threw all his clothes out the door and said if he didn't want to put them away he could live outside with the animals. Well, Abuela got angry at me! Can you believe it? He goes out to play, and I'm the one in trouble," Maria grumbled.

Captain John was silent for a moment before he turned to Maria. "How old is Jose?" he asked.

"You know he just turned nine. You were

there for the party," Maria replied crossly.

"Well, he's just a kid," Captain John said. "And both of you have had a tough year. Jose is worried and afraid, just like you. He's not sure when he'll see his mama and papa. You and Jose are in this together and you've got to stick together," the old man said firmly.

Maria just shrugged. Captain John looked off at the ocean and said, "I know for a fact that your parents are counting on you to stick together."

Maria turned to him sharply. "What do you mean?"

The old sailor looked away. "Why don't you talk to Ines about it tonight?" he suggested. Then he went back to fishing in silence.

When Ines returned that night from work, Abuela told her of Maria and Jose's fight. Ines called Maria into the room. "Are you going to punish me?" Maria asked.

"No, *niña*. There is something you should know. When it was time for you to leave Cuba, your parents thought that everything was in order. But at the last minute, some men at the airport told your father there was a mistake. Jose was not going to be allowed to leave since his visa waiver was not properly stamped. Of course, it was only a lie to get more money from your father. The point is, your parents refused to send you without Jose. Your parents knew you both would be better, stronger, if you were together," Ines said.

"They had heard that many brothers and sisters from the *Pedro Pan* Operation became separated when they arrived in the United States," she continued. "Sometimes the Americans who helped place the children could only take in one child. So, Maria, I know you're angry, but imagine how you would have felt if Jose wasn't with you. Be grateful that you didn't have to be alone."

After that, Maria and Jose still argued, but Maria tried to be a little more understanding. The summer was typically hot and humid. Since the tiny apartment was not air-conditioned, they spent most of their time on the beach. Maria began to plan for her birthday party with Abuela.

"I think I would like a beach party," she said one day at the beach. "Like the ones I see on Denise's television."

"That would be nice," Abuela replied. "You can invite Vilma, Denise, and some of the girls from school and ballet class. We'll have *bocaditos*, soda, and cake."

"Yes, sandwiches with all sorts of fillings, and I also want to invite Stephen and Alberto," Maria said, wriggling her toes in the sand.

Abuela looked up suddenly. "You want boys at your party?"

Maria nodded.

"*Dios mio!* You better talk to Ines," Abuela said nervously.

When they arrived home, Ines was not there. Maria thought it was strange, because Ines was working an early shift. "Let's start dinner, and I'm sure she'll be here soon," Abuela said. But Ines didn't arrive until after eight o'clock.

"What happened? We were so worried," Abuela exclaimed.

"I have so much to tell," Ines said breathlessly. "*Por favor*, a glass of water. I'm parched." After she drank two large glasses of water, Ines began. "I was just leaving work when Father Paul sent word he wanted to see me. I was nervous because I knew it had to be about Cuba."

"What is it?" Maria asked eagerly.

"Father Paul confirmed that your Mami and Papi and Miguel were able to get on board an American freighter and plead for asylum," Ines said in a rush.

"What is asylum?" Jose asked.

"It means they asked for refuge and protection," Maria responded in a dazed voice.

"*Sí*, and the captain granted it. They'll be here in two days," Ines said, as tears streamed down her face.

Jose jumped up and hugged Ines tightly. "It's

true. They're really coming!" he shouted.

Maria stood still, afraid to move, in case it was only one of her dreams. Ines looked at Maria and said, "*Niña*, it's over. Everything will be fine."

It came to Maria in a rush. At last they would be together! She began to cry. Mami and Papi were safe and finally coming! She didn't know what to do first. She hugged Ines and Abuela. And then she turned to Jose.

"Well, my *hermanito*, we made it," Maria said, hugging him. Jose held his sister. For once he was speechless.

The next two days passed quickly as they prepared for the reunion. Father Paul helped Ines find a two-bedroom apartment for Mami, Papi, Jose, and Maria. It was close to school and the beach. And as Maria and Jose packed up their belongings, they couldn't help but feel a little sad— sad to be leaving Ines and Abuela, and sad also that Tia Tati would be left behind in Cuba.

Maria looked at Abuela in the kitchen, finishing up her embroidery. Ines was in the bedroom, singing in Spanish as she polished the silver-framed wedding picture. Ines and Abuela had taken care of them, helped them, and, most importantly, loved them. Nothing that Maria could say would ever express how grateful she was to these two strong, generous women.

The night before the scheduled arrival, no one slept. Jose wanted to bring his Most Valuable Player trophy to the dock, and Maria insisted she wear her new full skirt that Abuela had made for her. Maria looked at her reflection in the mirror. Staring back at her were Mami's eyes.

Maria turned to Ines. "How do I look?"

Ines smiled at her. "You look perfect, Maria. Your parents will be so surprised at how much you have grown. And you, Jose, must have grown at least two inches. I bet you're almost as tall as your Papi." Jose beamed with pride.

They arrived at the dock by nine o'clock. It was a beautiful sunny day without a cloud in the blue sky. The port was nearly empty. Only work-men and a few stray cats seemed interested in what was coming in from the sea. Maria paced nervously. Jose couldn't keep still. He smoothed his trousers, fidgeted with his trophy—anything to keep busy.

Ines was just as anxious. She kept adjusting her hat and craning her neck to try to catch a glimpse of the freighter.

After what seemed like an eternity to Maria, they saw a large freighter turning into Biscayne Bay. Jose shouted, "It's them! I just know it!"

Maria held her breath as the freighter finally docked. They anxiously waited. Then Maria looked up at the railing and saw them. She caught her breath.

"Mami! Papi!" Maria yelled out.

They saw a white handkerchief waving from Mami's outstretched hand.

"*Niños!*" Mami yelled back. Maria and Jose began to run toward the plank. Before they could step foot on the ship, a large man in a dark suit stopped them. He wore a badge that said "Department of Immigration and Nationalization."

"Stop. I have some business to conduct first," the man said authoritatively.

Mami, Papi, and Miguel walked down the plank. Everyone stood still and watched nervously.

"Why are you in this country?" the man asked them as he examined their papers.

"We come here for asylum," Miguel responded.

"For freedom," Mami added.

The man looked at them and smiled. "Everything looks to be in order. Welcome to the United States. Your request for asylum has been granted." The man gave them their papers and the three happy people stepped across the yellow line.

Maria ran to Mami's open arms. Papi scooped up Jose and hugged him tightly. Then they changed places. Miguel took Ines in his arms and began to weep. He bent to hug Abuela. Soon they were all crying for joy. And then, as they wiped away their tears, they began to laugh.

"It's over, children. Never again will we be separated," Papi said, as he wiped Jose's face and his own.

"We're a family again," Mami said to her children through her tears.

Maria handed Mami her latest paintings. Mami stared at the pictures of Downtown, St. Rose of Lima, various buildings, and people Maria had met.

"That's Captain John and his granddaughter, Denise. They're my friends," Maria told her.

"I have so much catching up to do. Look at you, Maria, you've grown so much," Mami said, as she stroked Maria's hair.

"Yes, I've grown, Mami. And I've learned so much. We have so much to tell you," Maria said excitedly.

Ines and Abuela smiled at Maria. "There's no need to hurry, Maria. We have all the time in the world," Ines said.

As the group slowly walked away, holding hands, the seagulls swooped down and squawked. Papi looked around the nearly empty dock and said, "So this is Miami."

"No, Papi. There's much, much more to Miami," Maria said, as she held herself up very proudly. "It's our home now."

HISTORICAL POSTSCRIPT CHILDREN OF FLIGHT PEDRO PAN

Maria and Jose are fictional characters, of course, but their story is based on real events. Thousands of Cuban children *were* secretly flown to the United States when Fidel Castro seized control of the Cuban government.

Background

The Caribbean island of Cuba gained its independence in 1901. At first, Cuba did well, making money by exporting its sugar crop. But after world sugar prices fell, many Cubans experienced economic hardship.

Cuban democracy was very frail and weakened by widespread corruption. There were elections, but votes were bought openly. After 1933, a man named Fulgencio Batista dominated Cuban politics. When Batista became president in 1940, the government worked to improve the lives of poor Cubans, but landowners and their friends still dominated. Corruption worsened after 1946. Batista returned to power again in 1952 as a dictator, using violence to silence his enemies. Many Cubans began to seek change.

UPI / Bettmann

Fidel Castro, the leader of the Cuban Revolution, was a fiery, inspirational soldier and politician. His beard and cigars quickly became recognized trademarks.

In 1953, Fidel Castro, a law school graduate, led an armed attack on an army barracks. It failed, but after he was released from jail in 1956, he continued to fight in the Sierra Maestra Mountains. Castro's forces entered Havana on January 1, 1959, and ousted Batista.

At first, many cheered him. Castro promised to help the poor, to build schools and hospitals, and to limit the influence of the United States. In a decade, the number of teachers tripled. Education was made free and available to everyone through the university level. He took-

UPI / Bettmann

In 1961, the fate of the world hung in the balance as President John Kennedy faced down the Soviet Union over the issue of Soviet nuclear missiles based in Cuba. Both Cubans and Americans stayed glued to their television sets during the Cuban Missile Crisis

steps to end racial discrimination in Cuban life. Rents were lowered, and new housing built for those who formerly had to live in tenements.

But the new government also seized plantations, farms, factories, banks, and businesses from their owners. Claiming that his government was for the people, Castro took away the property of those who had lived well under Batista— people like the parents and relatives of Maria and Jose.

Taking Flight

Castro denounced those Cubans who had fled the island after his victory, calling them *gusanos* (worms). Now known as the "Commander," he invited the Soviet Union to provide aid, to buy Cuban sugar, and to defend the island. Castro declared himself a communist. On January 3, 1961, the United States broke diplomatic relations with Cuba, and later imposed an economic boycott on the island.

Three months later, Cuban exiles launched an attack at the Bay of Pigs, but it failed. Cubans hardened their anger at the United States. In October 1962, the Cuban Missile Crisis erupted when President John F. Kennedy insisted that the Soviet Union remove missiles from Cuban soil. The missiles were removed, but only after the world was brought to the brink of nuclear war. Throughout the Cold War period (1960-1989), relations between Castro and the United States remained tense, worsened by the fact that large numbers of Cubans fled the island for refuge in the United States, Mexico, and other countries.

A wave of affluent Cubans—professionals, business people, and landowners—departed their homes in the early 1960s, mostly for the United States (and mostly to South Florida). There they were assisted by religious and charitable organizations and by the United States government. Volunteers in the United States, led by the Roman Catholic Archdiocese of Miami, organized

Operation *Pedro Pan* to fly out a total of nearly 14,000 children who would be housed with relatives and volunteers until their parents could leave. Many came with only a few suitcases, like Maria and Jose, forced to leave most of their possessions behind.

Some were even less fortunate. These included those arrested for disagreeing with Castro's revolution, or for their philosophical or religious beliefs. Many spent long years as political prisoners in Castro's jails. But others, especially former peasants, embraced the Revolution.

Settling In

For those who wanted to leave, departing Cuba soon became much more difficult, especially after the Missile Crisis. Some, including people like Maria and Jose's parents, managed to get out by going to Europe or other Latin American countries and then gaining entrance to the United States. South Florida, especially Dade County (where Miami is located), became the haven for Cuban-Americans.

But conditions on the island worsened after the death of communism in Eastern Europe and in the Soviet Union in 1989. Cubans lacked spare parts for cars, trucks, and buses; they had to pay high prices for imported petroleum; consumer

UPI / Bettmann

Miami in the early 1960s. Many of the signs on the side of this market are in Spanish. Almost immediately, Cuban immigrants to Miami began to establish a vibrant cultural community that recalled their homeland.

goods and medicines became hard to get; people found it hard to find food. Fidel Castro blamed the economic troubles on foreign powers, especially the United States for its continued boycott.

Those Cubans, like the Aleman family in this book, who began life over in Miami would have had to work very hard. But life probably would have improved in time. Most of the Cubans who came to the United States after Castro's victory prospered, especially if they had been affluent in Cuba. Many of the new Cuban-Americans became very successful in just a few years and became highly influential in American politics. By the early 1990s, Cuban-Americans had been elected to Congress and to the mayor's office in Miami.

Other Books of Interest

Bucuvalas, Tina. *South Florida Folklife*. University Press of Mississippi, 1993.

Chavez, Jorge, trans. *As We See Moncada*. Havana: Gente Neuva, 1975.

Gernand, Reneé. *Cuban Americans*. New York: Chelsea House, 1988.

Grenquist, Barbara. *Cubans*. New York: F. Watts, 1960.

Lasaga, Jose I. *Pages from Cuban History*. Tr. Nelson Duran. Miami: Revista Ideal, 1984.

Levine, Robert M. *Cuba in the 1850s*. Gainesville: University Press of Florida, 1990.

Santana, Francisco. *Cuban Roots*. Hialeah, FL: Arca Publications, 1987.

Postscript written by Robert M. Levine, Professor of History and Director of Latin American Studies at the University of Miami. He has written seventeen books on Latin America, including two on Cuba.